MW00873077

WORKIN' AT THE WHALE WASH

Adapted by D. Finn

ISBN: 0-439-64153-5

DreamWorks' Shark Tale TM & © 2004 DreamWorks L.L.C.

Published by Scholastic Inc.
SCHOLASTIC and associated logos
are trademarks and/or registered trademarks
of Scholastic Inc.

12 11 10 9 8 7 6 5 4 3 2 1   4 5 6 7 8/0

Printed in the U.S.A.
First printing, September 2004

SCHOLASTIC INC.

New York   Toronto   London   Auckland   Sydney
Mexico City   New Delhi   Hong Kong   Buenos Aires

Oscar is a little fish with big dreams. One day—his lucky day—he's going at be at the top of the reef. But until then, he's working at the Whale Wash. . . .

Wash
Me!

Angie is Oscar's best friend. Her job is to answer the phone, "Sykes' Whale Wash. You get a whale of a wash, and the price—oh my gosh!"

When Oscar gets to work . . .
The Whale Wash starts thumping,
And the soapsuds start pumping.

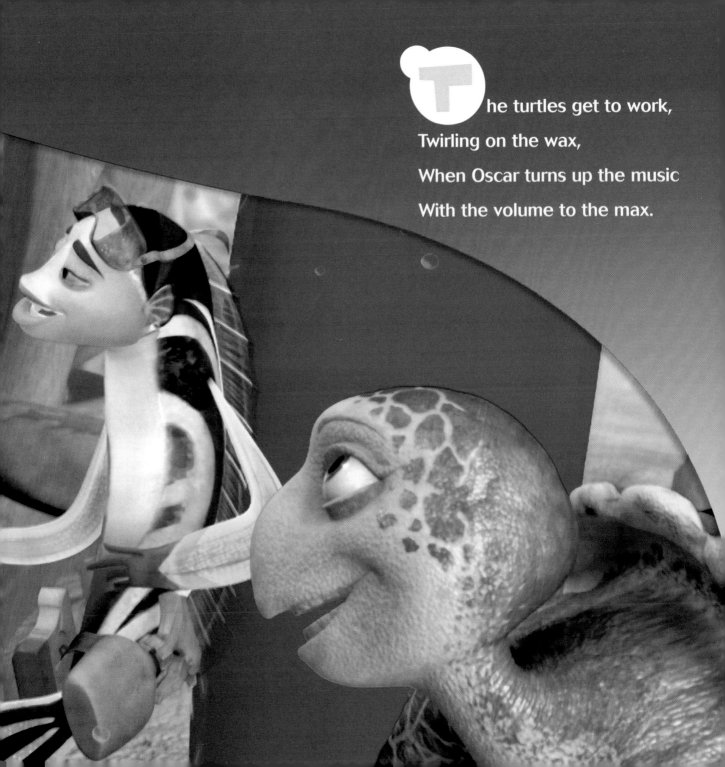

The turtles get to work,

Twirling on the wax,

When Oscar turns up the music

With the volume to the max.

The eels have the sparks
To keep the current glowing.
Intensified, electrified,
They keep the groove a-flowing.

The whales keep on moving
Through each and every station.
And the fish crew keeps on cleaning
While dancing in formation.

Angie is in the office.
She twists and shakes her fins.
While Gino cleans the blowhole,
He slips and slides and spins.

The scrubbers fall in line,

Dancing side by side,

Picking up the groove,

And scrubbing as they glide.

The crabs leap from bungee cords,
Snapping with their claws,
Removing all the barnacles
From the whales' scaly jaws.

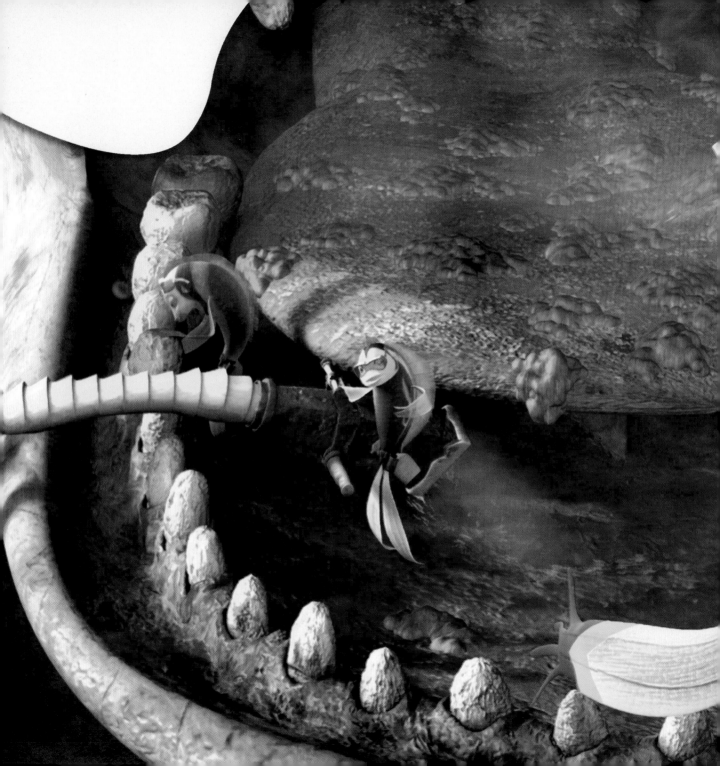

Inside the whale's mouth
It's dirty, green and slimy.
So Oscar works his magic,
To make it nice and shiny.

Johnson is the DJ
Way up in the booth.
He keeps the music pumping
While Oscar turns it loose.

Oscar may be a little fish,
But he's turning up the heat.
He's got the Whale Wash workin'
To an Oscarlicious beat!